Let's Go Traveling
in
MEXICO

The feathered serpent columns from the
Temple of the Warriors, Chichén Itzá

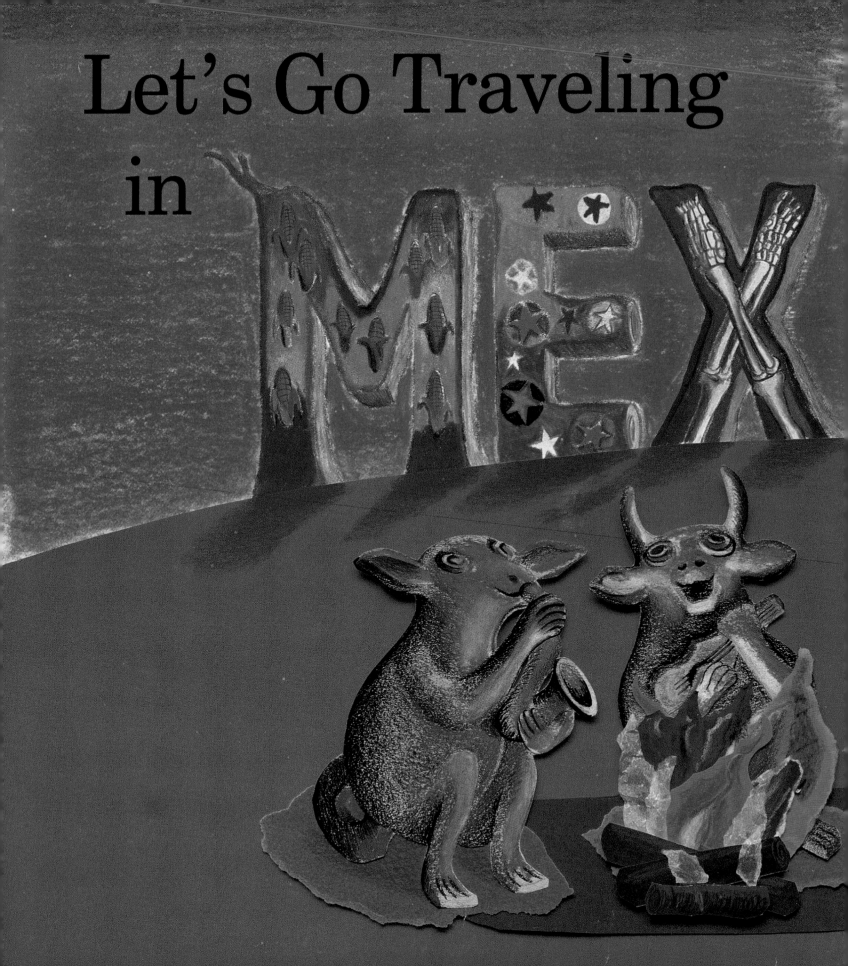

Let's Go Traveling in MEX

¡CO

Written and illustrated by
Robin Rector Krupp

Morrow Junior Books
New York

For the
young artists
of Mexico,
with
admiration
for those
who came before

The author gratefully acknowledges: Josefina Aguilar, Dr. Anthony F. Aveni, Rocky Behr and the staff of the Folk Tree in Pasadena, Ruth Lercher Bornstein, Jane Jordan Browne, Luis Covarrubias, Tom Owen Edmunds, Dr. Susan Toby Evans, Betty Green, Kara Knack, Dr. E. C. Krupp, Gabriel Fernandez Ledesma, Anita Linn, the *mariachi* musicians of Bazaar del Mundo in San Diego, Manuela Matute, Joan Menuey, and Chloë Sayer. The poster depicting the vision of *La Virgen de Guadalupe* is published by Cromos y Novedades de Mexico.

Pastel, colored pencils, black ink, and white paint were used
on white and colored papers for the full-color collage illustrations.
The text type is 14-point Century Schoolbook.

Library of Congress Cataloging-in-Publication Data
Krupp, Robin Rector.
Let's go traveling in Mexico/written and illustrated by Robin Rector Krupp.
p. cm.
Summary: Describes a trip through Mexico guided by Quetzalcóatl,
the feathered serpent, and celebrating each season of the year.
ISBN 0-688-12367-8 (trade)—ISBN 0-688-12368-6 (library)
1. Mexico—Description and travel—Juvenile literature.
[1. Mexico—Description and travel.]
I. Title. F1216.5.K78 1996 917.204'835—dc20 95-18206
CIP AC

Welcome!
¡Bienvenidos!

am Mexico's feathered serpent. For thousands of years my people have told stories about me. My splendor comes from the quetzal bird. My power comes from the *cóatl*, or snake. Put both names together and call me . . .

. . . Quetzalcóatl (ket-sahl-KO-ah-tl). My name slithers along your tongue. Let me guide you through my land. We'll celebrate each season as we travel through a year. Let's go to Mexico! Or as we say in Spanish, *¡Vamos a México!*

ABRIL

MAYO

JUNIO

JULIO

AGOSTO

MARZO

FEBRERO

ENERO

DICIEMBRE

NORTH
AMERICA

Atlantic Ocean

Mexico

SOUTH
AMERICA

Pacific Ocean

ANTARCTICA

SEPTIEMBRE

OCTUBRE

NOVIEMBRE

We'll start in January. Don't worry about the cold. Mexico is in the southern part of the continent of North America. Even in January, the sun will warm our backs. Mexico has thirty-one states, each one worth visiting. We'll start in Mexico City, the capital of them all.

United States

California
Arizona
New Mexico
Texas

Baja California
Sonora
Chihuahua
Coahuila
Nuevo León
Tamaulipas

Baja California Sur
Sierra Madre Occidental
Sinaloa
Durango
Zacatecas
San Luis Potosí
Sierra Madre Oriental

Gulf of California

Nayarit
Aguascalientes
Guanajuato
Querétaro
Hidalgo
Mexico City

Jalisco
Michoacán
Estado de México
Tlaxcala
Veracruz

Colima
Guerrero
Morelos
Puebla
Oaxaca

Gulf of Mexico

Río Grande

Maya carvings of a royal man and woman of Yaxchilán, now in the National Museum of Anthropology in Mexico City

The memories and magic of Mexico await us. So, hold on tight to my feathers. We fly to a land between two oceans, zoom between two mountain ranges, and soar more than one mile above the sea. *¡Mira!* Look, two volcanoes! And there is Mexico City, the biggest city in the world . . . *la ciudad más grande del mundo.*

Everywhere, the old exists beside the new. That's the story of Mexico. In Mexico City, the Plaza of Three Cultures tells it best. The remains of an Aztec temple sit beside a Spanish church and skyscrapers.

Friendly Mexicans greet us. Almost all speak Spanish, and many speak English, too. Some speak languages you may never have heard. Fifty-three different groups of Indians live in Mexico, and each group has its own language. But most people in Mexico are *mestizos*, mixtures of Indian and Spanish.

OLMEC

ZAPOTEC

MAYA

TEOTIHUACAN

2400 B.C. 2200 B.C. 2000 B.C. 1800 B.C. 1600 B.C. 1400 B.C. 1200 B.C. 1000 B.C. 800 B.C. 600 B.C. 400 B.C. 200 B.C. 0 A.D. 200 A.D. 400 A.D. 600

An Olmec colossal head, carved in stone without metal tools. Some of these heads are 8 feet high and weigh 40,000 pounds, 1000–600 B.C.

A Zapotec bat god mask carved from jade, A.D. 200–900

A Maya priestess sculpture made from clay, from the island of Jaina, A.D. 600–900

A Teotihuacán sculpture of the goddess Chalchiuhtlicue, Lady of the Waters. Carved from stone, A.D. 250–650

Mexico City's museums are some of the best in the world. Let's ride the modern subway to the National Museum of Anthropology. We Mexicans are proud of our heritage. Like a *sarape* blanket or *rebozo* shawl, we're woven together with many different threads.

AZTEC

TOLTEC

SPANISH

TOTONAC

MIXTEC

A.D. 800
A.D. 1000
A.D. 1200
A.D. 1400
A.D. 1600
A.D. 1800
A.D. 2000
A.D. 2200

A Mixtec food vessel, made from clay, A.D. 200–900

A Spanish crown, probably worn by a statue of the Virgin Mary. Made from silver, around A.D. 1700

A Totonac stone replica of equipment worn by ballplayers, A.D. 600–900

A Toltec column in the shape of a warrior. Made from four blocks of stone and over 14 feet tall, A.D. 900–1100

The Aztec Calendar Stone is 12 feet wide and weighs 40,000 pounds. Carved in basalt stone, it tells the Aztec story about the beginning of the world, A.D. 1400–1500

Teotihuacán

Pyramid of
the Moon

Pyramid of
the Sun

Teotihuacán

Mexico
City

Let's head north out of Mexico City to the ancient city of Teotihuacán (tay-o-tee-wah-KAN). We'll climb the Pyramid of the Sun. Climbing is hard work, but think of all the hard work it took to build a huge pyramid. Now we climb the smaller Pyramid of the Moon.

Two thousand years ago, Teotihuacán was the biggest city in the western half of the world. The Teotihuacanos (tay-o-tee-wah-KA-nose) ruled over other cities and traded with distant parts of Mexico.

We travel down the long Avenue of the Dead. At the remains of the Temple of Quetzalcóatl, I am carved into stone. Ancient legends say that I brought peace and culture. On my back is a mask that looks like Tláloc (TLA-lok). The legends say he brought storms and rain for the crops. I think he looks like corn, our most important food.

Remains of the
Temple of Quetzalcóatl

Detail of front facade of the
Temple of Quetzalcóatl,
with plumed serpents,
shells, and masks that
look like Tláloc,
the Rain God

The Avenue
of the Dead

The Citadel

Remains of the
Temple of Quetzalcóatl

Now, in late winter, the long finger of Baja (BAH-ha) California beckons us. We fish for marlin, yellowfin tuna, and bonito, then relax on the beach. At San Ignacio Lagoon we hire a guide, Alfonso, and his boat. Gray whales have migrated south to give birth in the warmer waters.

"Can we see them?" we ask Alfonso.

"*Sí, por supuesto.* Yes, of course. Whales were never hunted here, so the mother whales trust us."

¿Qué pasa? What's happening? A whale is coming toward us. She tries to rub the barnacles off her back by scraping against the bottom of our boat!

Hasta luego, Alfonso. We say good-bye and fly southeast across the mountains. An ocean of trees awaits us on the flat Yucatán Peninsula.

We want to be at the Maya site of Chichén Itzá (chee-CHEN eat-ZAH) for the equinox, or the beginning of spring. As many as 1,500 years ago, the Maya were great builders and astronomers. When they built Chichén Itzá, the Maya planned a display of light and shadow that tells a story about me. They called me Kukulcán.

El Castillo, Chichén Itzá

We arrive at Chichén Itzá in time for the March equinox. We learn that everywhere on earth, around the twenty-first of September and March, the length of night equals the length of day. This is called the equinox. On those days, the sun rises exactly east and sets exactly west. These times and directions were important to the Maya.

Now the setting sun hits the stepped edge of the pyramid called El Castillo (el kas-TEE-yo), or the castle. We join thousands of people to watch triangles of light shine on the only stairway with serpent heads. The zigzag shadow of a serpent moves slowly down the side! The Maya said that this was how I first came to earth, by descending from the sky.

Deep inside this pyramid, jade eyes glow on a jaguar throne. Jaguars still roam in the rain forest jungle. Are you brave enough to go there?

The jaguar throne inside El Castillo

Follow me on the narrow jungle trails. *¡Silencio!* Keep a lookout for poisonous snakes! *Escucha.* Listen. It's the high-pitched noise of insects. Sniff. A jaguar might be near. We're close to the ancient Maya ruin called Yaxchilán (yahsh-chee-LAN). Plant roots try to strangle the ancient stones. We spot a giant *ceiba*, or kapok, tree. The Maya said these trees held up the sky. *¡Qué buena suerte!* What good luck! We've seen some of the many plants and animals that live only here.

At night in our tents, we hear loud, deep, scary sounds. Was that the earth gasping for a breath? No, it's howler monkeys calling back and forth.

For days we raft on the Usumacinta (ou-sue-ma-SIN-tah) River, the highway of the Maya. We float along the southern edge of Mexico and the border of Guatemala. *¡Hola!* Rapids churn up ahead!

Pyramid of the
Niches, El Tajín

In June, we travel to El Tajín (el ta-HEEN), near the Gulf Coast. Here in the hot lowlands, the Totonacs built a city 1,300 years ago. We celebrate the longest day of sunlight, the summer solstice, and watch an ancient dance. Four men, called *voladores*, revolve thirteen times around a pole. They are hanging upside down! Some say the dancers are birds flying through cycles of days and years.

Folklórico dancers entertain us. The *mariachis* in their wide *sombreros* sing. Trumpets, violins, and fat guitars remind us: *vive, ríe, ama,* or live, laugh, love. Colors swirl during the day and fireworks explode at night.

Uno, dos, tres, cuatro, cinco, seis, siete, ocho. Already it's August, the eighth month. In a bus, we wind over bumpy mountain roads, traveling northwest. Our destination, Alamos, is one of many colonial towns founded when Mexico was a colony of Spain. In 1520, the Spanish conquered Mexico. They ruled for 300 years, and Spanish influences still remain. To pass time on the bus, we each try to spot things that originally came from Spain.

Ya llegamos. Now we arrive at the central plaza, with its beautiful church. Today, most people in Mexico are Catholics. This religion was also brought from Spain. Inside the dark church people pray and light candles. In many cities, Catholics honor their local saints, and all over Mexico, Catholics honor *La Virgen de Guadalupe*. This vision of the Virgin Mary, mother of Jesus, is said to have appeared to an Aztec Indian in 1531.

The plaza of Alamos, an old silver-mining town

La Virgen de Guadalupe

. . . and don't forget, *nosotros hablamos español.*

You forgot the wheel!

Speaking of that, we had a flat tire!

¡Qué lastima! What a pity!

Let's visit my friends, the González family, in Monterrey, one of my country's biggest cities. We gather at the end of summer, on September 16, which is our Independence Day. In 1808, a brave Catholic priest, Father Hidalgo, started the War of Independence. He carried the banner of *La Virgen de Guadalupe* and declared that Mexico must be free from Spain. The war lasted until 1821. Today, we remember the men and women who fought for freedom. Mexico is now a republic with a president elected every six years.

¿Tienes hambre? Are you hungry? Señora González pats cornmeal into *tortillas* and cooks them. We devour them, fresh and warm. Our feast includes foods and flavors that are native to Mexico—turkey, corn, tomatoes, avocado, pumpkin, coconut, chocolate, and vanilla.

¡Y los jalapeños son muy picantes! And those jalapeño (hah-lah-PAYN-yoh) chili peppers are very hot!

Statue of Father Miguel Hidalgo

Large painting of
Emiliano Zapata
by Diego Rivera

Fall brings the start of a new school year. Let's join students in Cuernavaca on a field trip to the palace of Hernán Cortés, the Spanish conqueror. Now the palace is a museum filled with Mexican art. Here, the students show us a mural painted by Diego Rivera in 1930. He was one of our most famous artists. The students point out Emiliano Zapata, a hero from this area. He stands beside his beautiful white horse.

At lunch, the children tell us about their school. They know that public education was started in 1860, by Benito Juárez, a Zapotec Indian who became president of Mexico. And guess what? They have homework, too! As we leave, we say, *"Muchas gracias."* They say, *"De nada."* We all say, *"Buen viaje,"* or "Good journey."

Yes, he wanted the peasants to be able to own their land.

Emiliano Zapata fought for changes in the government around 1910.

Diego Rivera is well known for his murals.

The island of Janitzio in Lake Pátzcuaro. A giant statue of the Revolutionary War hero Father José Morelos is at the top of the hill.

Now we fly to Lake Pátzcuaro (POTZ-kwa-roh), where we watch Tarascan Indians use their butterfly-shaped fishing nets. It is the end of October, time to celebrate *El Día de los Muertos,* the Day of the Dead.

We take the ferry over to the island village of Janitzio (HA-nit-zee-o). Sugar skulls greet us. We eat special breads, some baked in the shape of bones. Altars, paper decorations, and sculptures of silly skeletons are everywhere. All over Mexico, Indian and Catholic customs blend together as the living honor the dead.

Some people sprinkle paths of marigold petals that lead to indoor altars. They believe that the spirits of the dead follow the paths back to the comforts of home.

At the cemetery, we wait up all night, candles flickering along with our memories. All our lives we dance with death.

By the end of November we've bargained with our *pesos* for souvenirs and gifts from all over Mexico. We buy more in the town of Oaxaca (WAH-ha-ca), which is famous for its artists.

A street vendor named Rosa calls out, *"¡Mira! Hecho a mano. Mucho trabajo."* "Look! Made by hand. Much work."

Lake Pátzcuaro

Oaxaca

21

LA MANO

Yo soy el Aventurero

MI CASA ES SU CASA

Contiene Puré de Tomate, Agua, Chile Cebollas, A Sal y Espec

Many Mexicans create with whatever material is handy. Coconut shells become masks. Tin cans become toy trucks. Here's a twig. Does a gazelle or a monster want to come out of it?

And sometimes we paint designs on everyday objects. We say, "This is useful. It deserves to be decorated." In this way, we celebrate our daily life.

Long winter nights wrap around us at the end of our trip. We look forward to *fiestas* celebrating light in the midst of darkness. *"Feliz Navidad,"* we call out. "Merry Christmas." The lovely city of Guanajuato (guah-na-WAH-toe) welcomes us. We join *las posadas,* candlelight processions going from door to door, night after night. Like Mary and Joseph in Bethlehem 2,000 years ago, we look for a room. People turn us away, but finally someone invites us in. *¡Entren!* Warmth, shelter, *tamales, chocolate caliente,* and a star-shaped *piñata* wait for us.

To make this *piñata,* an artist has molded papier-mâché around a clay pot or balloon. We each try to break it. Everyone gets three whacks.

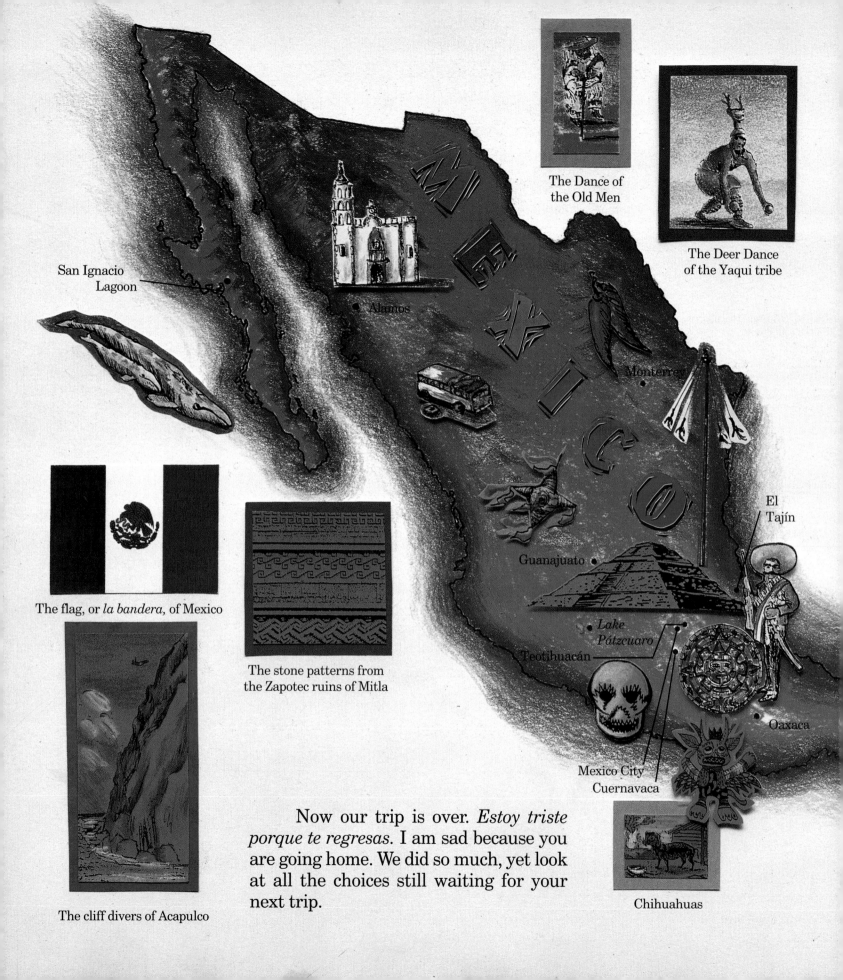

The Dance of
the Old Men

The Deer Dance
of the Yaqui tribe

San Ignacio
Lagoon

Monterrey

El
Tajín

The flag, or *la bandera,* of Mexico

The stone patterns from
the Zapotec ruins of Mitla

Alamos

Guanajuato

*Lake
Pátzcuaro*

Teotihuacán

Mexico City
Cuernavaca

Oaxaca

Chihuahuas

The cliff divers of Acapulco

Now our trip is over. *Estoy triste
porque te regresas.* I am sad because you
are going home. We did so much, yet look
at all the choices still waiting for your
next trip.

Soccer games

Quetzalcóatl from the Toltec capital of Tula

Jai alai games

Migrating butterflies

We exchange *abrazos,* or big hugs. I whisper a secret in your ear. The warrior Toltecs ruled the city of Tula 1,000 years ago. They said that I, Quetzalcóatl, became the planet Venus so that I could travel with the sun. When I rise with *el Sol,* I am called the Morning Star. Sometimes I am the Evening Star, the first bright one that you see. You can make a wish on me and . . .

The floating gardens of Xochimilco

Chichén Itzá

Usumacinta River

Yaxchilán

Armadillos

Charro rodeo riders

Back-strap loom weavers

The Quetzal Dance

The Maya ruins of Palenque

. . . remember my beautiful country.
¡Adiós, amigos, adiós!